Contents

Cheer
Challenge

illustrated by Tuesday Mourning

text by Ronda Redmond

raintree

a Capstone company — publishers for children

Raintree is an imprint of Capstone Global Library Limited, a company incorporated in England and Wales having its registered office at 264 Banbury Road, Oxford, OX2 7DY – Registered company number: 6695582

www.raintree.co.uk
myorders@raintree.co.uk

Art Director: Heather Kindseth
Graphic Designer: Kay Fraser
Illustrated by Tuesday Mourning
Originated by Capstone Global Library Ltd
Printed and bound in China

ISBN 978 1 4747 3229 1
20 19 18 17 16
10 9 8 7 6 5 4 3 2 1

British Library Cataloguing in Publication Data
A full catalogue record for this book is available from the British Library.

We would like to thank Chris Kreie, Media Specialist at Eden Prairie Schools, MN, USA, and Mary Evenson, Middle School Teacher at Edina Public Schools, MN, USA, for their invaluable help in the preparation of this book.

For Tori and Sammy, my subject matter experts. Thank you for keeping me honest, and keeping me excited.

Chapter 1

The vote

Amanda Reynolds stared at the blank square of paper in her hand. She couldn't decide what to write. Who should she vote for? Who should be the captain of the year seven cheerleading squad?

She thought about what her best friend, Rachel, had said. "You should totally vote for yourself, Amanda. I'll vote for you and almost everyone else will, too. You'll win for sure."

But Amanda wasn't sure. It didn't seem right to vote for yourself for cheerleading captain.

The other girls were passing their votes to their coach. It was time to make a decision.

Amanda started writing her own name. But then she quickly scribbled it out.

She looked up. Everyone else was finished. She hunched over the paper to make sure no one could see her. Then she wrote "Rachel".

Before she could change her mind, she folded the paper. Then she handed it to Miss Wall, the cheerleading coach.

"So?" Rachel's freckled face popped up in front of Amanda's.

"So, what?" Amanda asked.

"So, who did you vote for?" Rachel asked, smiling. She put her hands on her hips. "I voted for you, and you better tell me you did the same," she added.

"Well, you know, I just didn't know if it was right," Amanda said.

Rachel rolled her eyes. "Whatever, Amanda," she said. "You and I both know you would make the best captain. No one else here could handle it." She looked behind her to make sure no one was around. Then Rachel whispered, "Come on, Amanda, tell me! Who did you vote for?"

The rest of the squad began to gather around Miss Wall.

"Hey, we better get over there," Rachel said. "Looks like she's about to announce who won."

All eight members of the year seven Cougar cheerleading squad stood in front of Miss Wall, waiting to hear what she would say.

The coach held up a gold star pin. Every year, the captain of the squad wore the special pin.

"I'm about to tell you who will wear this on her uniform," Miss Wall said. "The captain will be a leader to you, but she is not the only one responsible for the success or failure of your season. You are a team. Don't lose sight of that."

Then Miss Wall said, "This year's captain will be. . ."

The pause seemed to last forever. She looked at each girl. Then she held her hand out to Amanda.

Finally, Miss Wall said, "Your captain this year will be Amanda."

Rachel yelled happily and jumped up and down. Chloe and her best friend, Courtney, leaned towards each other and started whispering. The other girls clapped.

Amanda smiled down at the star in her hand.

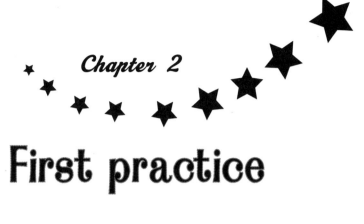

Chapter 2

First practice

The next day, Amanda showed up for practice a few minutes early. She quickly changed into her uniform.

Then she went into the gym. She was excited for her first practice as captain.

Miss Wall was already on the floor, stretching. Amanda was glad to see her friendly face.

"Hey there, Amanda," Miss Wall said. "Are you ready for the first practice?"

Amanda smiled. "Definitely," she said.

She sat down to start her own stretches. At cheerleading camp, she had learned to ease carefully into a stretch. With her legs pointed out in front of her, she reached down to grab her toes and held the pose as she counted to 30.

"Good," Miss Wall said, "because here comes your squad."

Amanda looked up. All the other girls were trailing out of the changing room. Amanda started to feel nervous.

Yesterday, she had been excited to be voted captain. It meant that the other girls liked and respected her. But now she was going to have to act like a captain. She was going to have to lead the squad. What would that be like?

"Okay!" called Miss Wall. "Grab a piece of floor and get ready to stretch. Amanda, get us started."

The girls spread out on the gym floor. Amanda took a deep breath. She looked over at Rachel. Rachel gave her a huge smile and a double thumbs-up.

"Okay," Amanda began. "Let's all start in a straddle position." She watched as the other girls followed her lead.

Then she went on, "Push it out as far as you can without hurting. Making sure your back is straight, lift your hands straight up. Turn to face your right foot. Now, bend over your right leg."

Near the back of the group, she saw Chloe and Courtney whispering to each other.

"Chloe and Courtney," Miss Wall said sternly, "this is not social hour." Then she nodded at Amanda. "Keep going, Amanda."

Amanda nodded back. "Okay. Now, take the stretch as far as you can and hold. Don't bounce. You'll hurt yourself." Then Amanda began counting to 30. But she saw Chloe in the back of the group, rolling her eyes at Courtney.

As Amanda held her stretch, she closed her eyes. Being the captain was already harder than she'd thought it would be.

Chapter 3

Grace under pressure

The Cougars' first game was just two days later. The girls would be doing their routine during halftime of the basketball game.

The first half of the basketball game was almost over. Amanda eyed the clock as it ticked down the seconds. Finally, the buzzer sounded and the basketball players ran off the court.

"Let's go!" Amanda said.

There was a knot in her stomach. She led the squad out to the middle of the gym.

The squad had only had two practices, and Amanda knew their routine wasn't strong enough yet. Miss Wall had insisted that they perform at the first game of the season anyway.

The cheerleaders formed two lines. They stood in Ready Stand position. That meant that their feet were together and their hands were at their hips.

The crowd went quiet. Amanda plastered a smile on her face, and hoped the rest of the girls did, too.

At a card table set up near the entrance to the gym, the music guy was digging through a pile of CDs, looking for their music.

Finally, the music guy popped a CD into the stereo. But when the song started, Amanda's heart sank.

It was the wrong song.

She didn't know what to do. The other girls were looking at her.

Panicked thoughts ran through Amanda's mind. Should they try to do the routine to the wrong song? Would that even work?

Out of the corner of her eye, Amanda saw Miss Wall run over to the stereo. She turned off the song.

The silence felt like a huge weight pressing down on Amanda. Her smile left her face.

The other girls were frozen. They were nervously waiting for the music.

Amanda knew she had to do something. So she looked into the stands and shouted, "Ready? Okay!"

She slapped her hands to her thighs in Clean position. Somehow, the other girls knew to follow along. And a few seconds later, the music started.

After the routine was over, the squad ran to the sidelines. Amanda was relieved to be done with the routine.

"That was what they call grace under pressure!" Miss Wall said as they huddled around her. "Well done!"

"It didn't look so graceful from where I was standing," said Ruby.

"Yeah," said Anna. "From the back, I saw a lot of sloppy arms. Plus, we didn't land our last jump at the same time."

"We have a lot of work in front of us," said Miss Wall. "We need to tighten up our moves. But today, you worked together as a squad. You followed Amanda perfectly. Today was a great first step!"

Amanda smiled and looked down at the star pin on her uniform.

Chapter 4

Inspiration?

The next day at practice, the girls worked hard for two hours. Amanda led the team through their routine three times in a row.

She felt like it was starting to be really good. They just needed to keep practising.

With fifteen minutes left of practice, Amanda knew they had time to do the routine again. "One more time, from the top," she said, clapping her hands.

She walked towards the CD player to start the song again. Most of the squad groaned.

"My arms feel like rubber," said Anna.

"My legs feel like lead," said Ruby.

"If you want me to do that routine again, you're going to have to scrape me off the floor first!" said Rachel.

Amanda stared at them. "Come on, you guys," she said. "Do you want to get better or what? We've come a long way on this routine. I think we're getting really close. We have ten minutes left of practice. Let's just do the routine one last time."

"Or we could do some yoga," Miss Wall suggested.

Their coach loved yoga. She'd taught the cheerleaders some poses that felt great after a long practice.

The girls let out a sigh of relief. They started to roll out the yoga mats, which Miss Wall always stacked against the wall before practice.

Amanda looked at Miss Wall with a pained expression. If anyone should understand the need for more practice, it should be their coach. But the coach just met Amanda's gaze and gave her a wink.

Miss Wall led the cheerleaders through a series of yoga poses to stretch their legs, shoulders and backs.

After fifteen minutes of yoga, the girls seemed more relaxed. They rolled the mats back up and left the practice room.

Amanda waited until the others left. Then she quietly said, "Miss Wall, can I talk to you?"

Miss Wall smiled at her. "Sure, Amanda," Miss Wall said. "Let's talk while we put these mats in the storage room."

They each grabbed some mats and headed down the corridor. Miss Wall asked, "What's on your mind?"

Amanda took a deep breath. "Well, it's the squad," she admitted. "I mean, do you think we're doing okay? I think the routine still needs a lot of work, and I don't understand why we didn't run through it one more time."

They shoved the mats into the storage closet. Miss Wall locked the door.

"You have a lot of spirit, Amanda," she said. "You have high standards and you want the squad to perform well. But you can't be a leader by pushing people."

Amanda, embarrassed, looked down at the floor. "I never meant to push anyone," she said quietly.

"I know you didn't," Miss Wall said. "Look. You have all of the energy and drive and heart it takes to be a good captain. But the other half of being a captain is being an inspiration to the other girls, making them want to be better. You have to figure out just how you'll inspire them."

Amanda frowned. Miss Wall smiled at her. "Give it time. I'm sure you'll think of something," she said.

Chapter 5

Something new

Amanda couldn't stop thinking about what Miss Wall had said. She thought about it as she walked home. And she thought about it at dinner with her family.

Amanda needed to figure out a way to inspire the other cheerleaders. But how? She couldn't think of anything to do.

After dinner, she checked her email. There wasn't much. It was mostly junk. But one of the messages caught her eye.

Amanda belonged to a group called Teen Cheer, which often sent out emails to its members about upcoming events.

Usually, Amanda just skimmed those emails. But the subject of the email in her inbox was "Competitions: The Ultimate Cheer Challenge."

So she opened it. The email read,

CHEER YOUR WAY TO VICTORY! TRY SOMETHING NEW. COMPETE!

A cheerleader's number-one job is to cheer sports teams to victory. But that's not all a cheerleader does. At a cheerleading competition, the audience screams for you!

Cheer competitions are the ultimate combination of skill, teamwork and pride!

Sign your squad up now for a cheer competition near you. Get inspired by other squads, be surrounded by talented cheerleaders at all teen levels and cheer your way to victory!

There was a list of locations for competitions.

Amanda gasped. One of the competitions was in Larksville. That was just a few kilometres away!

The competition was four weeks on Saturday. That wasn't much time, but Amanda just knew her squad could do it if they tried hard enough.

She followed a link in the email. When she clicked on it, she found a website with the competition information.

Quickly, Amanda printed out all the information she could find. She planned to bring it to Miss Wall the next day.

Amanda was thrilled. This could be the perfect way to inspire the squad!

Chapter 6

Put it to a vote

At school the next day, Amanda made copies of the information she had printed about the competition. She stashed the copies in her locker until the school day was over. As soon as the bell rang, Amanda headed for Miss Wall's office.

She knocked timidly on the door. Miss Wall opened it, smiling. "Hey, Amanda!" she said. "What's up? Shouldn't you be getting ready for practice?"

Amanda bit her lip. Then she said, "You know how you said I needed to inspire the team? Well, I found something. I think it could be the perfect challenge for us."

"Come on in," Miss Wall said. "Tell me all about it."

* * *

At practice, Amanda handed out the copies she'd made of the information. She hoped the competition would sound cool to the other girls.

Everyone sat, reading quietly. Amanda waited for someone to speak.

Finally, Miss Wall broke the silence. "So? What do you think of Amanda's idea?" she asked.

"I don't know," Ruby said. "This is only a month away. That's not enough time."

Anna added, "We would need a whole new routine. My cousin and I went to a cheerleading competition last summer, and they had huge mounts, throws and falls. We don't have time for that."

"Anna, that was a university cheerleading contest. That's way different from this," Amanda told her.

"Amanda's right. University competitions are different," Miss Wall said, nodding. "There are safety rules you need to follow at all cheerleading competitions. University squads can do all of that fancy stuff. We can only do mounts to a certain height, and we don't do throws or falls. There are a number of rules we'll have to follow."

"What fun is that?" Anna asked, tossing the piece of paper to the ground.

"The fun is in thinking creatively," Amanda answered. "We have to follow the rules, but after that our only limit is our imaginations."

"I think we should do it," said Rachel.

Then something shocking happened. Chloe slowly nodded her head. "I think so, too. I mean, we have a lot of really good ideas. Look at all of the changes we made to our regular routine."

"Exactly," said Rachel.

"Let's vote," said Miss Wall. "Raise your hand if you want to do the competition."

Amanda took a deep breath. She held up her hand.

Slowly, all the other girls raised their hands. A huge smile swept across Amanda's face.

"Well, I guess it's official," Miss Wall said. "We're entering the competition!"

They all clapped and cheered. Then everyone started talking at once.

"Hey! Guys, hold on a second," Amanda shouted. "There are a couple of things we have to talk about if we're going to do this." She pulled a pile of papers out of her backpack. "The rules aren't just about how high our mounts can go," she went on. "There's more to it than that."

"Like what?" asked Anna.

"Well, practice, for one," Amanda said.

"They tell us how we have to practise?" asked Ruby. "That's weird."

"No, not how to practise," Miss Wall answered. "We just have to agree that we will practise as a squad."

Amanda nodded and said, "Ruby, you were right when you said that we didn't have much time. We only have a month to practise. I think we're going to have to schedule some extra practice time."

"I think that's a good idea," said Rachel.

"No problem," said Ruby.

"But there's a catch," added Amanda. "Well, sort of a catch. They have a rule that all members of the squad have to attend all of the practices. If you miss even one, you can't be in the competition."

"What if you get sick?" asked Rachel.

"You can miss one practice, if you have a doctor's note," said Amanda.

The girls looked a little upset. Amanda started to feel nervous. Did they hate the idea now?

Miss Wall held up her hand. "This competition is about teamwork," she said. "The point of it is not just to compete as a team. You have to practise as a team, too. As the captain, Amanda will be in charge of taking attendance at every practice. When we get to the competition, she will have to turn that sheet in. The judges will not bend on these rules."

Amanda smiled and said, "Let's start by figuring out when we can all meet. Then we can get down to the real work."

She pulled a calendar out of her bag and put it on the floor. The other girls gathered around.

Chapter 7

Making changes

Over the next two weeks, the team worked hard at perfecting their routine. But Amanda felt it still wasn't quite right.

"Okay, everyone line up and get in Ready Stand position. Let's go again, from the top," Miss Wall said.

"Why do we have to start in Ready Stand?" asked Chloe, frowning.

"All routines start like that at this school," said Ruby.

"Well, what if we all started in Clean position? That would be cool," said Amanda. "Instead of hands on our hips, we'd have straight arms at our sides."

Chloe shook her head. "Actually, I was thinking of something a little different," she said. "We always start standing in two boring lines."

"That's because we're one squad. We should all look the same," said Amanda. "We need to look polished. That's what the judges look for."

Chloe frowned and said, "We look polished when we start moving through the routine. The changes we've made are really good. I think it's almost perfect. But it does seem like something is missing." She looked at Amanda. "It came to me last night," she said. "I think I know what we need."

"What?" asked Amanda.

"I think we should start the routine as individuals!" Chloe explained.

"Isn't it getting a little late for changes?" said Rachel. "The competition is less than two weeks away. Plus, we have to cheer at three more games between now and then. We have enough to worry about without making more changes."

"I agree," Amanda said.

"Let me show you what I mean. Then decide if it's too much, okay?" Chloe asked.

Miss Wall said, "Go ahead, Chloe."

"Picture this," Chloe said. "We're all standing out here, before the music starts. Only, instead of standing in lines, we're standing in a circle."

"With our backs to the judges? I don't like that," Rachel said, crossing her arms and frowning.

Chloe sighed. "No," she explained. "We stand facing out. And instead of arms down or hands at our hips, everyone's arms are a little bit different."

Ruby said, "That sounds sloppy!"

"Yeah, it does," Anna said.

Amanda stood up and turned to face the other girls. "We all agreed to work together on this and to think creatively," she said, putting her hands on her hips. "That means listening to each other's ideas."

She sat back down and looked to Chloe. "Go ahead. We're listening," Amanda said. "Tell us your idea.

Chloe gave her a little smile.

Then Chloe took a deep breath. She explained, "Okay, so we're in a circle, facing out, and the girl in the very back has her arms in an open High V. Each girl next to her has her arms in a V, but not as high. The girl at the front of the circle has her arms down, in a Low V."

"The girl in the very back could have straight knees, and the girl in the front could have bent knees," said Anna. "We would look like a sun, like our arms were the rays!"

"Hey, I like that," said Miss Wall.

"So, we're all a little different, but we come together to make one thing," said Amanda. "I get it." She smiled.

Chapter 8

A little glitch

Everything was going perfectly. The new opening to the routine was awesome. All the girls agreed that it would really impress the judges.

By the time the competition was less than a week away, the routine was almost perfect. Four more days of practice would do it. They would be flawless. Every detail would be just right.

Amanda couldn't wait.

On the Tuesday before the competition, Amanda was hurrying to practice when Rachel ran up to her.

"Amanda, I have a favour to ask you," Rachel said. She gave Amanda her sweetest smile.

"What's up? Let's walk and talk or we'll be late to practice," Amanda told her.

"Here's the deal," said Rachel. "My aunt is coming to visit. Her flight comes in on Friday."

"That's the day before the competition," added Amanda.

"Right," Rachel said. "The day before. It's not a huge problem, just a tiny little glitch."

"Glitch?" Amanda asked. She stopped walking and looked at Rachel.

"Yeah," Rachel said. "A tiny one. See, I found these awesome boots online and my mum said I could get them if I saved up enough money to pay half."

"Okay," Amanda said.

Rachel smiled. "Well, I finally saved up enough money. And there's a shopping centre by the airport that has those boots."

Amanda sighed. "Get to the point, Rach!" she said with a laugh.

Rachel laughed, too. "Okay, okay. Anyway, my mum said we could stop at the shopping centre before we pick up my aunt. I really want to, but that would mean I'd miss the last practice."

Amanda felt shocked. She said, "Rachel, you know you can't miss practice and still compete."

Rachel looked away from her. "Yeah, I know," she said.

Amanda asked, "Are you saying those boots are more important than the squad?"

"Of course not!" Rachel exclaimed. "The squad is way more important."

"Then what are you saying?" asked Amanda.

Rachel rolled her eyes. "I'm saying that as my best friend, you could excuse me from practice and tell everyone that I had a doctor's appointment," she said quietly.

Amanda gasped. "You're asking me to lie for you?"

Rachel said, "It's just a tiny lie. Besides, it's not like we'll need another practice. We have the routine sorted."

"I can't do that, Rachel," said Amanda.

Rachel frowned. Then she said, "It's just about you being able to boss everyone around, isn't it?"

Amanda felt like someone had punched her in the stomach. She stared at Rachel. Finally, Amanda asked quietly, "Is that what you really think?"

Rachel shrugged. "I don't know. You're different. You don't listen to me. It's like all you care about is winning the competition. You don't care about our friendship."

Amanda thought she might start crying. "Rachel, I do listen to you. You're my best friend," she said.

Rachel said, "Then listen to me now! Just do this tiny favour for me. After all, I helped you get elected as captain."

"I can't," Amanda said quietly. "I'm sorry, Rachel. I just can't."

Rachel stared at her. "Fine. Well, I guess that shows me how much you care about our friendship." Then she stomped down the corridor.

* * *

Rachel and Amanda didn't talk for the rest of the week.

On Friday before practice, Amanda waited by Rachel's locker, hoping her friend would show up. But she never did.

Amanda slowly walked to the changing room alone. She changed without talking to anyone else and went into the gym. Everyone was already there, except Rachel.

Miss Wall handed her the attendance sheet. Amanda stared down at it.

It had been almost perfect. Chloe had an important dentist appointment one afternoon, but she had gotten a note from her doctor. Besides that, every girl had attended every practice.

Until today.

Amanda glanced at the clock, hoping there would still be time for Rachel to come, but it was already 3.40 p.m. Practice had officially started ten minutes ago.

"Where's Rachel?" Ruby asked.

Amanda sighed. "I guess she's not coming," she said.

Miss Wall looked worried. "Do you think she'll get a doctor's note?" she asked.

Amanda stared at the ground. "No," she said sadly. "They don't give out doctor's notes when you go to the shopping centre."

"This is serious," Miss Wall said. "If Rachel's not coming, she can't compete on Saturday."

"I know," Amanda said. "She's not coming." She looked at the other girls. They all looked worried.

Amanda knew it was her job to be strong. So she said, "We're still going to compete, so let's get started!"

Chapter 9

The big day

On Saturday morning, the girls piled into a school van. Miss Wall drove them to the competition.

The competition was being held at a college that was only a few kilometres away. When they arrived, the huge stadium where the performances would be was full of cheerleaders of all ages. The littlest cheerleaders were only five years old. Amanda thought they were so cute.

Her squad was scheduled to perform fourth. They nervously watched as the first three squads performed their routines.

As the third routine ended, Amanda's stomach felt like it was tied in a million small knots. It was time.

The girls huddled up before they were called out to the floor.

"Okay, girls, this is it!" Miss Wall yelled over the sound of the crowd. She smiled and said, "You have all worked really hard."

She paused to look around the circle at each girl. Amanda tried to stop feeling nervous.

Finally, Miss Wall said, "I want you to know that, no matter what happens today, I am proud of you. Every one of you."

Amanda thought their coach did look really proud. She smiled at Miss Wall.

The girls squeezed together for a group hug. Just then, Amanda felt someone grab her arm and wiggle into the huddle.

It was Rachel.

Frowning, Miss Wall said, "I'm sorry, Rachel, but rules are rules. You can't compete with us."

Rachel looked down at the floor. "I know," she said quietly. "I'm not here to compete. And I'm really sorry. It was a stupid decision to make."

Amanda didn't know what to think. What was Rachel doing?

Rachel looked up and went on, "I just wanted to be here. I woke up this morning and I felt terrible."

She looked at Amanda and smiled nervously. "I wanted to come cheer you on," Rachel finished.

Amanda smiled and gave her a squeeze.

"So, you're here to cheer on the cheerleaders?" asked Chloe.

The girls all laughed. Rachel laughed, too. "Yeah. I guess that's the reason I'm here. Everyone needs a cheerleader, right?" she said.

"Right!" said Miss Wall. "You can watch from the sidelines with me, Rachel."

Then the announcer's voice blared over the loudspeaker. "Ladies and gentlemen, please welcome the Cougars!"

The girls put their hands together and shouted, "One! Two! Three! I have you, and you have me!"

Before she could break the huddle, Rachel put her arms around Amanda. She whispered into Amanda's ear. "Go get 'em, captain. You rock!"

Amanda felt the knots in her stomach relax. She had her best friend back.

The girls headed out to the floor. They formed their starting pose.

Amanda's heart was beating really hard. She took a deep breath in and then slowly let it out.

The music began.

The crowd was just a blur to Amanda. She hardly realised that they were there.

Instead, she felt the energy of the squad. Their arms moved together. Their legs kicked up to the exact same height and at the exact same angle.

It was almost magical.

Their hard work had all come to this. Amanda felt proud.

When the music ended, the girls held their ending position. The crowd exploded with clapping and cheers.

Amanda's heart was pounding and she was sweating. All she cared about was that she could see Miss Wall and Rachel on the sidelines, screaming happily and jumping up and down.

And when the results were announced later that day, the team pushed Amanda forwards to receive the trophy for first place.

About the author

Ronda Redmond lives in a small town in Minnesota, USA, with her husband, Jim, her sons, Sam and Charlie, and her dogs, Georgie and Frank. She studied creative writing in college and now works in the business world as an analyst and writer. She loves to read, cook and make pottery.

About the illustrator

When Tuesday Mourning was a little girl, she knew she wanted to be an artist when she grew up. Now, she is an illustrator who lives in Knoxville, Tennessee, USA. She especially loves illustrating books for kids and teenagers. When she isn't illustrating, Tuesday loves spending time with her husband, who is an actor, and their son, Atticus.

Glossary

announce say something officially or publicly

captain leader of a team

challenge something that is difficult to do. Challenge can also have another meaning: if you challenge someone, you invite them to try to do something difficult.

competition contest

flawless perfect

glitch sudden problem

inspiration if someone is an inspiration to another person, they inspire, or make the other person want to do better

position the way in which someone is standing

qualities characteristics, or ways of being

routine set performance

yoga system of exercises, stretches and meditation that helps people become relaxed and physically fit

Cool tips for
cheerleading competitions

When you **arrive** at the competition

- Stay calm! Competitions are fun, exciting and stressful.

- Look over the facilities so everyone knows where everything is.

- Check the schedule and make sure all squad members know where they are suppose to be and when.

- Be polite! Your behaviour reflects not only on you but on the whole squad.

- Be supportive of other squads.

- Make mental notes or even jot down things you think might help your squad next time.

- Be positive.

- Have fun.

When you **get back** from a competition

- Have a squad meeting and critique your performance. Talk about what worked and what didn't.

- Look at any videos or pictures that were taken. Learn from them.

- Make sure all criticism is helpful. Remember, you're a team and you're only as good as your weakest member. Your goal should be to improve as a squad, not to alienate people or make them feel bad.

- Once you've rehashed the competition and learned from it, put it behind you and move on to your next one.

Comprehension questions

1. There were good things and bad things about being captain of the cheerleading squad. What were the hardest things for Amanda? What were some of the positive things about being captain?

2. Rachel asks Amanda to make an exception for her to get out of practice. What would you do if you were in Amanda's position? Talk about ways that Amanda could have responded to Rachel.

3. In the beginning of this book, Amanda has to decide if she's going to vote for herself for captain. What would you have done? Talk about it.

Writing prompts

1. Are you on any teams or squads with your friends? If you and a friend have an argument, how does it affect your team? Write about a time an argument with a friend affected your team. What did you do to solve the problem?

2. At the end of this book, Amanda and her squad have a successful competition. Write about a success you have had in your favourite sport. What happened? How did it make you feel?

3. Miss Wall tells Amanda that she needs to find a way to inspire her teammates. Can you think of any other ideas Amanda could have had to inspire her team? Write about some ideas.

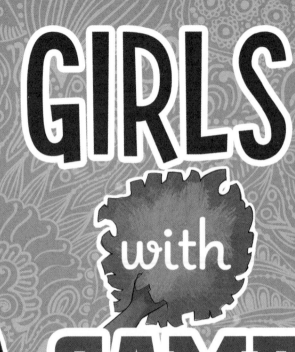

GIRLS

with

GAME

READ MORE
SPORT STORIES

SPORT STORIES
HORSEBACK
Hurdles

SPORT STORIES
Gymnastics
JITTERS

SPORT STORIES
Running
SCARED

SPORT STORIES
Cheer
CHALLENGE

SPORT STORIES
FOOTBALL
SURPRISE

SPORT STORIES
DANCE
DILEMMA

THE FUN DOESN'T STOP HERE!

Discover more

Sport Stories at

www.raintree.co.uk